D1630077

993688702 6

THE ROBOT BOP

Level 6D

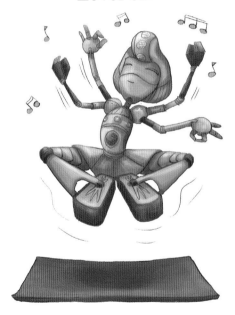

Written by Lucy George
Illustrated by Caroline Romanet

What is synthetic phonics?

Synthetic phonics teaches children to recognise the sounds of letters and to blend (synthesise) them together to make whole words.

Understanding sound/letter relationships gives children the confidence and ability to read unfamiliar words, without having to rely on memory or guesswork; this helps them to progress towards independent reading.

Did you know? Spoken English uses more than 40 speech sounds. Each sound is called a *phoneme*. Some phonemes relate to a single letter (d-o-g) and others to combinations of letters (sh-ar-p). When a phoneme is written down it is called a *grapheme*. Teaching these sounds, matching them to their written form and sounding out words for reading is the basis of synthetic phonics.

Consultant

I love reading phonics has been created in consultation with language expert Abigail Steel. She has a background in teaching and teacher training and is a respected expert in the field of synthetic phonics. Abigail Steel is a regular contributor to educational publications. Her international education consultancy supports parents and teachers in the promotion of literacy skills.

Reading tips

This book focuses on two sounds
made with the letter o: o as in hot
and oa as in cold.

Tricky words in this book

Any words in bold may have unusual spellings or are
new and have not yet been introduced.

> ### Tricky word in this book:
>
> **nervous**

Extra ways to have fun with this book

After the reader has read the story, ask them questions
about what they have just read:

Where does Ro bop?
Can you do The Robot Bop?

I just want to dance!

A pronunciation guide

This grid contains the sounds used in the stories in levels 4, 5 and 6 and a guide on how to say them. /a/ represents the sounds made, rather than the letters in a word.

/ai/ as in game	/ai/ as in play/they	/ee/ as in leaf/these	/ee/ as in he
/igh/ as in kite/light	/igh/ as in find/sky	/oa/ as in home	/oa/ as in snow
/oa/ as in cold	/y+oo/ as in cube/music/new	long /oo/ as in flute/crew/blue	/oi/ as in boy
/er/ as in bird/hurt	/or/ as in snore/oar/door	/or/ as in dawn/sauce/walk	/e/ as in head
/e/ as in said/any	/ou/ as in cow	/u/ as in touch	/air/ as in hare/bear/there
/eer/ as in deer/here/cashier	/t/ as in tripped/skipped	/d/ as in rained	/j/ as in gent/gin/gym
/j/ as in barge/hedge	/s/ as in cent/circus/cyst	/s/ as in prince	/s/ as in house
/ch/ as in itch/catch	/w/ as in white	/h/ as in who	/r/ as in write/rhino

Sounds this story focuses on are highlighted in the grid.

/**f**/ as in phone	/**f**/ as in rough	/**ul**/ as in pencil/hospital	/**z**/ as in fries/cheese/breeze
/**n**/ as in knot/gnome/engine	/**m**/ as in welcome/thumb/column	/**g**/ as in guitar/ghost	/**zh**/ as in vision/beige
/**k**/ as in chord	/**k**/ as in plaque/bouquet	/**nk**/ as in uncle	/**ks**/ as in box/books/ducks/cakes
/**a**/ and /**o**/ as in hat/what	/**e**/ and /**ee**/ as in bed/he	/**i**/ and /**igh**/ as in fin/find	/**o**/ and /**oa**/ as in hot/cold
/**u**/ and short /**oo**/ as in but/put	/**ee**/, /**e**/ and /**ai**/ as in eat/bread/break	/**igh**/, /**ee**/ and /**e**/ as in tie/field/friend	/**ou**/ and /**oa**/ as in cow/blow
/**ou**/, /**oa**/ and /**oo**/ as in out/shoulder/could	/**i**/ and /**ai**/ as in money/they	/**c**/ and /**s**/ as in cat/cent	/**y**/, /**igh**/ and /**i**/ as in yes/sky/myth
/**g**/ and /**j**/ as in got/giant	/**ch**/, /**c**/ and /**sh**/ as in chin/school/chef	/**er**/, /**air**/ and /**eer**/ as in earth/bear/ears	/**u**/, /**ou**/ and /**oa**/ as in plough/dough

Be careful not to add an 'uh' sound to 's', 't', 'p', 'c', 'h', 'r', 'm', 'd', 'g', 'l', 'f' and 'b'. For example, say 'fff' not 'fuh' and 'sss' not 'suh'.

Ro is a little Robot.
She loves to bop.

She dances to hip-hop, non-stop!

Wherever Ro goes, she bops.
She bops to the shops...

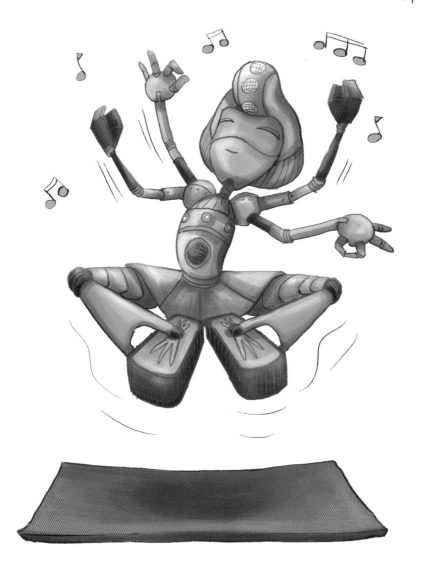

she bops while she jogs...
she even bops doing yoga!

Ro has made up a dance called
The Robot Bop and one day
she wants to do it on a proper
dance floor.

But what's this? Ro has been invited to a party! Ro's never been to a party before, but she knows there will be a dance floor. And that means...

...she can do The Robot Bop!

Ro arrives at the party feeling
wobbly with excitement.

She can't wait to do The Robot
Bop on a proper dance floor!

The moment the music starts,
Ro trots to the front and begins
The Robot Bop.

But at that moment, the others
totally stop. Ro is the only one
dancing.

Everyone is goggling at her.
Ro feels **nervous**. She wobbles...
then topples... and stops!

"Don't stop!" they cry.

Do they like The Robot Bop…?

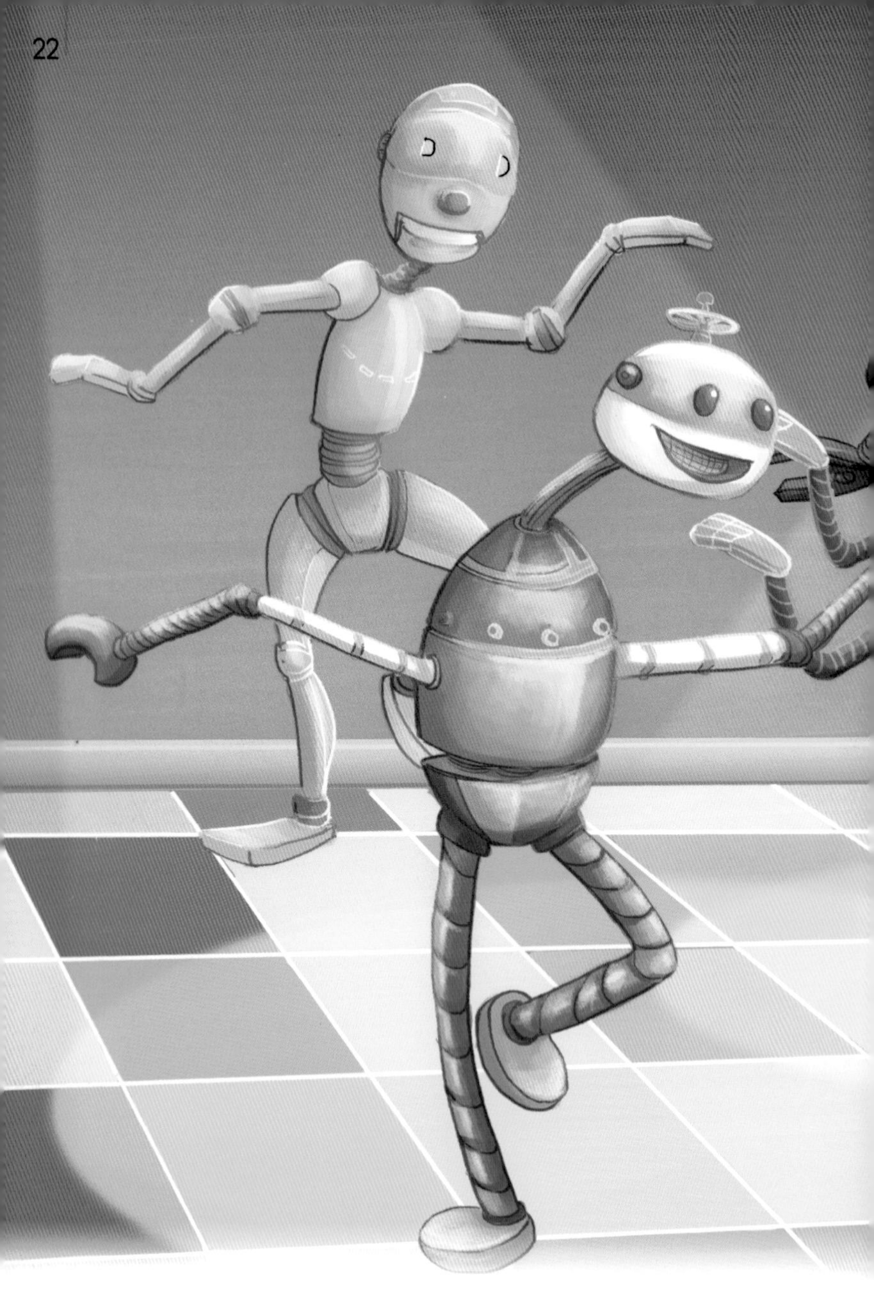

They love The Robot Bop!

They love it so much,
they can't stop!

OVER **48** TITLES IN SIX LEVELS
Abigail Steel recommends...

Some titles from Level 4

I love reading phonics — The Maze — 978-1-84898-559-9

I love reading phonics — Fairy Fay's Bad Day — 978-1-84898-560-5

I love reading phonics — Pirate School — 978-1-84898-566-7

Some titles from Level 5

I love reading phonics — Snapped by Sam — 978-1-84898-561-2

I love reading phonics — Max's Trip — 978-1-84898-562-9

I love reading phonics — George the Genius Gerbil — 978-1-84898-567-4

Other titles to enjoy from Level 6

I love reading phonics — What Wally Wanted — 978-1-84898-563-6

I love reading phonics — Superhero Ed — 978-1-84898-564-3

I love reading phonics — Adine's Igloo — 978-1-84898-569-8

An Hachette UK Company
www.hachette.co.uk

Copyright © Octopus Publishing Group Ltd 2012
First published in Great Britain in 2012 by TickTock, an imprint of Octopus Publishing Group Ltd,
Endeavour House, 189 Shaftesbury Avenue, London WC2H 8JY.
www.octopusbooks.co.uk

ISBN 978 1 84898 570 4
Printed and bound in China
10 9 8 7 6 5 4 3 2 1